RUDOS
ROO-dohs

"Tough guys" who bend or break the rules

NIÑO

LAS HERMANITAS

LA LLORONA

LA MOMIA DE GUANAJUATO

EL CHAMUCO

Match dedicated to
Moni Blast and Octavio el Dialéctico de la Justicia

Copyright © 2016 by Yuyi Morales
A Neal Porter Book
Published by Roaring Brook Press
Roaring Brook Press is a division of Holtzbrinck Publishing Holdings Limited Partnership
175 Fifth Avenue, New York, New York 10010
mackids.com

Library of Congress Cataloging-in-Publication Data

Names: Morales, Yuyi, author.
Title: Rudas: Niño's horrendous hermanitas / Yuyi Morales.
Description: First edition. | New York : Roaring Brook Press, 2016. | "A Neal
    Porter Book." | Summary: "Niño's little sisters get in on the wrestling
    action"— Provided by publisher.
Identifiers: LCCN 2016004882 | ISBN 9781626722408 (hardback)
Subjects: | CYAC: Wrestling—Fiction. | Brothers and sisters—Fiction. |
    BISAC: JUVENILE FICTION / Sports & Recreation / Wrestling. | JUVENILE
    FICTION / People & Places / United States / Hispanic & Latino. | JUVENILE
    FICTION / Family / Siblings.
Classification: LCC PZ7.M7881927 Ru 2016 | DDC [E]—dc23
LC record available at https://lccn.loc.gov/2016004882

Our books may be purchased in bulk for promotional, educational, or business use. Please contact your local bookseller or the Macmillan
Corporate and Premium Sales Department at (800) 221-7945 ext. 5442 or by e-mail at MacmillanSpecialMarkets@macmillan.com.

First edition 2016
Book design by Andrew Arnold
Printed in China by RR Donnelley Asia Printing Solutions Ltd.,
Dongguan City, Guangdong Province

1 3 5 7 9 10 8 6 4 2

RUDAS
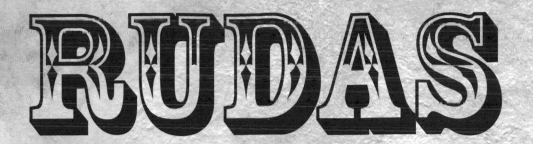

NIÑO'S HORRENDOUS HERMANITAS

YUYI MORALES

A NEAL PORTER BOOK
ROARING BROOK PRESS
NEW YORK

Everybody was minding their own business when . . .

SEÑORAS Y SEÑORES NIÑOS Y NIÑAS

The time has come to welcome the phenomenal, spectacular, legendary one of a kind . . .

~~NIÑO~~

¡LAS HERMANITAS!

Wrestling champions!
Lucha Queens!

The little sisters reign
supreme, cracking down
on their opponents with
incredibly rude feats.

Watch out, here comes
their first one!
BOOM, BOOM, BOOM!
The Poopy Bomb Blowout!

Such a rotten move!

In no time the **EL EXTRATERRESTRE** is gassed out of this world!

Gag!

¡Guácatelas!

CABEZA OLMECA is up next with his best Diaper Change, but no one expected Las Hermanitas' famous Nappy Freedom Break so early in the match!

FUZZZLASH!

Cabeza Olmeca's head is stunned!

EL CHAMUCO didn't see their next hideous move coming.

Tag Team Teething is Las Hermanitas' hot ticket to doom!

Preposterous!
Las Hermanitas escape
from dire straits
with the Twofer Tattle!

¡Madre!
Will anyone be spared
from their Pampered
Plunder?

But wait. What is that?

It is . . .

. . . a Look-and-Book Diversion. And they fell for it! Unbelievable!

Such a brotherly trick!

How will Las Hermanitas handle
this heartbreaking breakout?

With the Hula-boo-hoo!

Nothing this juicy
has happened since
last season's
Great Lemon Squirt.

What a wretched turn of events.
Not to mention twice as loud.

Can anyone make
them stop already?

What a Seize and Squeeze!
¡Sí, Señor!

TÚKURU-TRÚ

Las Hermanitas' strong hold is inescapable!
They are

RUDAS!